SHAKES BEAR
IN THE DARK

JOSHUA
KORNREICH

Sagging
Meniscus

Set in Mrs Eaves XL with LaTeX.

ISBN: 978-1-952386-28-2 (paperback)
ISBN: 978-1-952386-29-9 (ebook)
Library of Congress Control Number: 2021944564

Sagging Meniscus Press
Montclair, New Jersey
saggingmeniscus.com

For Leo—and a few others, I suppose

SHAKES
BEAR
IN
THE
DARK

SHE HAD BEEN DEAD for about a week, I think. Or maybe it was two weeks.

Not that a single one of them gave a shit, of course. Yet they were all there, crammed into that courtroom, every damn one of them, not because they *had* to be there, mind you—it's not like they all had been subpoenaed or anything like that—but because they *wanted* to be there, to bear witness to, and take pleasure in, my comeuppance.

I mean, it had been years—decades, even—since I had seen any of them, but I could still recognize all their faces, and I could still remember all their names.

Harry the Hippo.

Richard the Rhino.

Lenny the Lion.

Lyle the Leopard.

Chester the Chipmunk.

Eddie the Elephant.

Tito the Turtle.

Henry the Horse.

Benny the Four-Eyed Bunny.

Bucky the One-Eyed Bunny.

And, of course, there was the one-and-only William Shakesbear—he was in that courtroom as well. Shakesbear was the prosecution's star witness. There he was, clad in his creamy satin blouse, his purple silk trousers, and that adorable blue beret, with just enough of his deliciously red velvet skin showing to drive me bonkers. The prosecution had him sitting at the counsel table during the whole trial, surely just to get to me.

That Shakesbear—he was always a fucking tease.

While I never did see Kiki the Kangaroo over the course of the trial, I didn't need to see him to know that this court was a kangaroo court. After all, even the jury box was packed with only plush animals, no humans. I mean, whatever happened to having a jury of one's peers?

"All rise."

We all rose from our seats as the judge flew majestically into the courtroom, wearing that same sort of black robe that all presiding judges wear in real life and in the movies. He flapped his wings this way and that way, giving both Shakesbear and me a good, hard look, then perched himself on the bench, behind the broad podium and metal nameplate that said THE HONORABLE WISE O. OWL.

Judge Owl was a plush owl, and the robe he wore was sewn onto his neck. I wondered if it had been traumatic for him having it sewn onto his neck like that, or if sewing clothes onto a plush animal was more like the fleeting pain that a human being endures when getting stitches.

"You may be seated," hooted the judge. "So, yesterday, we heard witness testimony from the defense—the defendant's wife, his sister, his best friend from preschool, his first grade teacher, his middle school guidance counselor, his sleepaway camp counselor, his first sexual partner, his college roommate, his longtime business associate, his primary care physician, and his—am I missing someone here? Oh, right—and his pedicurist. So, today we'll hear a bit more witness testimony from the prosecution before winding things down. Do you have your list of witnesses, Counsel?"

The lead prosecuting attorney, like Shakesbear, was a plush bear. His name was Beary Scheck. I always hated Barry Scheck, the human attorney, but I think I hated Beary Scheck even more. After the O.J. trial, Beary Scheck became a very sought-after lawyer in several high-profile plush trials, but perhaps in the hopes of rewriting his dubious legacy, he began taking on cases in which the moral high ground was clearly on his side.

Scheck turned his big, furry head to whisper in Shakesbear's ear. His star witness whispered something back and made dramatic gestures with his arms.

"Counsel, do you have your list of witnesses?" repeated the wise, old judge.

"We do, Your Honor," Scheck replied.

"Alright then. You may approach the bench."

With a glancing smirk in my direction, Scheck walked up to the bench and handed Judge Owl the list. Judge Owl skimmed through the sheets of paper and handed a few of them back to Scheck who walked back to the counsel table.

I wanted to punch Scheck in the face. In the corner of my eye, I could see the bailiff watching over me like a hawk.

Or, excuse me—the Beariff. Those fucking teddy bears had me surrounded.

"The prosecution calls Mr. Bobby Banana to the witness stand," said Scheck.

Bobby Banana climbed over the rows of plush spectators and swung himself over the door of the witness stand. Scratching his armpit, the plush monkey took the oath.

Then Scheck started in.

"Mr. Banana," said Scheck, "when and how did you meet the defendant?"

"In 1982, sir. I was sitting on the racks of The Pied Piper toy shop at the Manhasset Miracle Mile, when a young boy swiped me from the shelf and squeezed me very hard. It just about knocked the wind out of me."

"This young boy to whom you're referring—he is now a grown man, is he not?"

"He is."

"And this grown man you speak of—is he in this courtroom today?"

"He is."

"Can you point to this man?"

"Yes, sir." Bobby pointed his finger at me with one hand while scratching the side of his neck with the other.

"Let the record show that the witness has pointed his finger at the defendant," said Judge Owl. "Proceed, Counsel."

"Thank you, Your Honor. Mr. Banana, does the defendant's presence make you anxious here to-day?"

"Yes, sir."

"I understand, Mr. Banana. We all do. Perhaps when this is all done, the court will be so kind as to treat you to some complimentary plush bananas to eat and— "

"Objection, Your Honor," said the plush bear sitting next to me. It was my defense attorney, Dominic Bearbara. He became a bit of a semi-celebrity in plush circles after his human likeness, Dominic Barbara, took on the Jessica Hahn and Joey Buttafuoco cases during the late '80s and early '90s, but then sort of fell off the grid when he became strung out on diet pills. After doing some time in rehab, he got his lawyer's license revalidated, and became a born-again Christian. He had shed plenty of poundage, yet he was still quite rotund. I had tracked him down after I heard an ad on the Howard Stern show that tried to sell him off for a substantial discount—a rather humiliating episode that seemed to leave him in the doldrums, but I think my case rejuvenated him.

He rose confidently, if unsteadily, from his chair, took a couple of deep breaths, then spoke: "The prosecution knows, just like everyone sitting here in this courtroom knows, that the witness has no functioning digestive tract, and is therefore incapable of taking advantage of such a bribe, even if such a bribe would be considered admissible in an ethical court of law such as this one."

"Sustained," said Judge Owl. "Mr. Scheck, proceed with caution. This is a courtroom, not a fruit stand."

The courtroom spectators chuckled at the judge's remark. Shakesbear raised his quill pen as if the plush owl's one-liner had just provided him with the perfect sonnet. He jotted whatever idea it gave him onto his legal notepad.

"So, Mr. Banana," said Scheck, "after the defendant bear-hugged you, disrupting your ability and your right to breathe, what happened?"

"His mother—may she rest in peace—she freed me from his grasp and carried me to the checkout register for purchase."

"And were you purchased, Mr. Banana?"

"Yes, I was purchased."

"And for how much were you purchased?"

"Thirteen ninety-nine."

"Thirteen ninety-nine, as in thirteen dollars and ninety-nine cents?"

"Yes, sir. Plus sales tax."

"And how much was that sales tax?"

"Back then, I think it was just over eight percent, but don't hold me to it."

"Fair enough, Mr. Banana—we won't hold you to it. Now, were you ever made aware of the fact that you were purchased, with the aid of a coupon, for twenty percent less than your list price?"

Bearbara shot up from his chair. "Objection, Your Honor. I don't see how the purchasing coupon of the deceased mother of my client is relevant to this case."

"Overruled," said the Wise Old Owl. "Let's wait and see where Mr. Scheck is going with this one."

"Thank you, Your Honor," said Scheck. "Mr. Banana were you ever made aware of the discount that devalued your intrinsic worth—a discount that was, in fact, applied to an expired, and therefore, invalid coupon?"

Bobby's voice cracked. You could tell this was news to him. "No, I—I wasn't aware of that."

"And were you ever made aware of the fact that just prior to this devaluing and denigrating purchase—for, after all, it wasn't like the human store owners were selling you at fair value to begin with—that the defendant had torn off the index finger of another plush monkey that was previously purchased from that same store—Chi-Chi the Chimp?"

"Chi-Chi-the-*Who*?" Bobby couldn't believe what he was hearing.

"Objection, Your Honor," said Bearbara, pushing himself up from his chair with great difficulty and heavy breathing. "The prosecution's characterization of Chi-Chi the Chimp, the defective plush chimpanzee it is now alluding to, was not anatomically torn in any way by my client. It has already been substantiated in court that Chi-Chi the Chimp always had four fingers on one of his hands, which was the unfortunate result of an in-factory manufacturing mishap. Also, the prosecution should show its witness a little more respect when they refer to my client's beloved Chi-Chi as a monkey, when in fact a chimpanzee is not classified in the plush animal kingdom as a plush monkey, as Mr. Banana is, but rather a plush ape."

"Sustained," said Judge Owl. "Mr. Scheck, the court advises you to abstain from careless misnomers and controversial nomenclature. As I've said all along, let's stick to the facts that have already been substantiated in this courtroom or in other courtrooms in prior proceedings."

"My apologies, Your Honor," said Scheck. "Mr. Banana, what happened after you were checked out at The Pied Piper?"

"Well, the cashier didn't stuff me in one of those plastic shopping bags, which was kind of nice, I suppose. So, when the defendant and his mother left the store, they just carried me out to the parking lot with their bare hands—I mean, the defendant did—and took me with them into their car."

"You mean the defendant's mother's car, correct?"

"Yes, that is correct, sir."

"This car they put you in—what kind of car was it?"

"I think it was a sky-blue '77 Dodge, but I'm not entirely sure about that. I mean, I didn't get to see many cars prior to my being purchased, so it was sort of difficult for me to identify what model it was."

"So, the defendant—the man whom you pointed your finger at in this courtroom, who back then was the young boy you described—he was still holding you when you all entered the car, correct?"

"That's correct."

"*How* was he holding you?"

"Under his shirt."

"He was holding you under his shirt?"

"Yes, sir."

"How so? Under the front of his shirt or under the back of his shirt?"

"Under the front."

"What kind of shirt was it?"

"I think it was a sweatshirt with Darth Vader on the front of it. I mean, if it wasn't Darth Vader, then at least it was somebody else with a spooky black helmet on his head that resembled Darth Vader."

"And was this in the front seat or the back seat where he was holding you under the front of his Darth Vader sweatshirt?"

"In the back seat, sir."

"Were you scared, Mr. Banana?"

"Yes, sir. Quite a bit."

"Did you ever think of why the defendant was doing this to you, holding you this way?"

"I don't know, sir. I really can't say. Because it felt good to him maybe? Or maybe—"

"What was the defendant's mother doing while you were being held under the defendant's Darth Vader sweatshirt?"

"She was driving the car. She had the radio on. She was listening to Neil Diamond, Christopher Cross—you know, music like that kind of music."

"Did she see what the defendant was doing with you under his sweatshirt?"

"I'm not sure, sir. Like I said, my head was under his sweatshirt."

"You probably had a lot of trouble seeing under the defendant's Darth Vader sweatshirt."

"Yes, sir."

"And you probably had a bit of trouble *breathing* under the defendant's Darth Vader sweatshirt, yes?"

"Yes, sir. A bit. Quite a bit. Yes."

"In fact, you probably sounded a bit like Darth Vader yourself under that Darth Vader sweatshirt."

"Sir?"

"You know, like the way Darth Vader sounds under his mask in those Star Wars movies? *Hawwww-herrrr . . . hawwww-herrrr*—like that."

Bearbara rolled his eyes and shot up again. His belly hit the edge of the counsel table on the way up, moving it a foot forward. "Your Honor—"

"Sustained," said the Wise Old Owl. "Mr. Scheck, don't make me warn you again about your dramatic antics. This is not a circus act. This is a criminal case in a criminal courtroom."

"Dramatic antics?" Scheck turned to the spectators sitting behind him. "And all this time I've been told I'm the most boring plush lawyer in the history of trial law."

The Wise Old Owl waited for the laughter in the courtroom to subside before speaking.

"Rest assured, Mr. Scheck, you *are* the most boring plush lawyer in the history of trial law," said the judge. "You may proceed, Counsel."

Scheck turned back toward Bobby. "Mr. Banana, to where did the defendant and his mother drive you?"

"To their house."

"Describe their house."

"It was a red house. A red house with black shutters."

"Was it a big house?"

"No, it was a small house. I mean, it had an upstairs and a downstairs, but it was a small house regardless, sir."

"So, you went into this small, red house with black shutters—was the defendant still holding you at this point?"

"Yes, sir, he was."

"*How* was he holding you?"

"By my throat, sir."

"Can you repeat that and speak up please."

"I said, 'By my throat.' Sir."

"By your throat. The defendant was holding you by your throat. Against your will, I imagine, yes?"

"Yes, sir."

"Where in the house did the defendant take you as he held you by your throat?"

"Upstairs."

"Upstairs to where?"

"Upstairs to his bedroom."

"Can you describe the defendant's childhood bedroom please?"

"Yes, sir. It had a bed—a twin bed. It also had a closet. A window. And a bunch of posters on the walls."

"Posters, huh? And what were on these posters on the defendant's walls?"

"Some of them had men on them with makeup on their faces, and they were holding electric guitars in their hands as if they were gunslingers or something."

"Gunslingers?"

"Uh-huh. Gunslingers."

"What else did you see on these posters?"

"Well, there was also one with a coffin on it."

"A coffin?"

"Yes, sir."

"You mean like a coffin to hold a corpse inside?"

"Well, it was like one of those ancient Egyptian kind of coffins—like the kind you find in one of them big tombs. You know, like for kings or pharaohs or something."

"Kings or pharaohs?"

"Uh-huh. And I think the coffin that was on his poster was the one for King Tutankhamun."

"King Tutankhamun? You mean King Tutankhamun as in King Tut?"

"Yep, that's the one, sir. King Tut. Uh-huh."

"And King Tut is dead, is he not?"

"Yes, I believe so, sir."

"Do you think the defendant thought he was King Tut or some kind of pharaoh or something?"

"Objection, Your Honor," said my bloated attorney. "How is the witness supposed to ascertain my client's thoughts and feelings?"

"Sustained," said Judge Owl.

"Fair enough," said Scheck. "Mr. Banana, this dead man in this ancient coffin, this King Tut you speak of—he was on a poster on the defendant's wall, you said."

"Uh-huh. That's what I said, sir."

Scheck went back to his counsel table and retrieved what looked like a small billboard. He returned to the witness stand with the billboard and held it up so Bobby and everyone else in the courtroom could see it.

It was the floor plan of my childhood bedroom.

"So, this wall that the poster was on—was it next to the window here or by the door over there—where was it?"

"It was here." Bobby pointed his finger at the spot. "It was above the bed."

"Above the defendant's bed, you say?"

"Yes, sir."

"How did this make you feel, Mr. Banana—this poster of a dead man in his coffin, hovering right above the defendant's pillow? Did it make you feel like you were in *grave* danger?"

Bearbara shot up again. "Objection, Your Honor. The witness's feelings are hardly the issue here."

"Yes, hardly," said Judge Owl. "But I'm going to overrule nonetheless. Proceed, Mr. Scheck."

"Mr. Banana," said Scheck. "On that day you were inside the defendant's bedroom for the first time, did you feel threatened at any point, or that perhaps your well-being might be in jeopardy?"

"Yes, sir. I did feel that way."

"And, besides pillows and blankets, etcetera, what did you see on the defendant's bed during that first time you were inside his bedroom?"

"Well, it was dark in there that first time. Very dark. But on the bed, I could see other plush animals."

"Other plush animals?"

"Yes, sir."

"Are any of those plush animals here in this courtroom today?"

"Yes, sir."

"How about the plush animal who's been sitting next to me at the counsel table over there—Mr. Shakesbear. Was Mr. Shakesbear on the defendant's bed that first time you were inside the defendant's bedroom?"

"Yes, sir, he was."

"And how did he look to you? What condition was he in?"

"He looked tired. Tired and depressed. Very depressed."

"What about his clothes—how did they look?"

"They looked wrinkled. Wrinkled and rumpled."

"Rumpled, you say?"

"Uh-huh. Rumpled. And his beret was crooked."

"Crooked?"

"Yeah, like it was dangling on his head by a single stitch or something."

"Did Mr. Shakesbear say anything to you when he saw you during that first encounter?"

"Yes, he did."

"What did he say?"

"He said, 'We have seen better days.'"

"Did he say anything else?"

"Yeah. He said, 'I have not slept one wink.'"

"Not one wink, he said?"

"Yeah, that's what he said—not one wink. And then he said, 'I am a man more sinned against than sinning.' And then he said something like: 'He hath eaten me out of house and home,' or something weird like that."

"I see." Scheck turned around for a moment to face me before turning back to Bobby. He was enjoying every minute of this. "So, what happened after the defendant put you on his bed? Did he say or do anything with you or any of the other plush animals?"

"No, he just placed me on the bed next to the others, shut his bedroom door behind him, and went downstairs."

"So, it must have been quite dark in the room when he left you—even darker than when you first entered, correct?"

"Correct, sir. It was dark. Very dark."

"And when you were left in the dark of the defendant's bedroom, did you or any of the other plush animals say or do anything while the defendant was downstairs?"

"No, sir. No one said or did a thing. I think everyone was too scared to say or do anything."

"Why were they scared?"

"At that point, I wasn't sure."

"How long were you all sitting in the dark there?"

"For about an hour or so, I'd say."

"Did you hear anything from outside the room while you were in the dark?"

"Yeah, some talking, some footsteps. Some doors slamming. Some yelling. Some crying, too, at times."

"Some yelling and crying, you say?"

"Yes, sir."

"Was some of this yelling and crying coming from the defendant?"

"Yes, sir. I mean, I didn't actually see him yelling or crying, but I could tell it was him because it sounded like a little boy yelling and crying, and there was only one little boy living in that house, so it had to be him."

"You mean it wasn't like some other little boy on the TV or radio or something else?"

"No, sir. It was him. I'm certain."

"And what was the defendant yelling or crying about?"

"It was hard to tell from where I was in the dark upstairs, but it sounded like it was something about sauce and spaghetti."

"Sauce and spaghetti?"

"Yes, sir. Something about how he wanted cheese and not sauce, or something."

"Could you make out anything else the defendant was yelling or crying about?"

"Yeah, there was this one other thing: He said something about taking a bath. Or maybe not taking a bath? Like he didn't want to take another bath for the rest of his life, or something like that."

"Uh-huh. Got it," said Scheck. "But, eventually, the defendant came back up the stairs to his bedroom to where you and the other plush animals, including Mr. Shakesbear, were sitting there scared-stiff in the dark—is that correct?"

"Yes, sir. That's correct."

"So then what happened?"

"Well, he turned on the light, and started changing into his pajamas, and—"

"Hold on a moment there, Mr. Banana. Did you just say that the defendant started to change into his pajamas?"

"Yes, sir."

"You mean that he started to take his clothes off in front of you and the other plush animals without saying a word?"

"Pretty much. I mean, I think he was sort of pretending to talk like a robot under his breath, saying something about 'making holes in teeth' or something like that, but I'm not entirely certain about exactly what it was that he was saying."

"Can you please describe how the defendant's naked body looked as he undressed in front of you and the others?"

"Yes, sir. It was kind of pasty-looking. Pasty and bony."

"And can you describe the pajamas that the defendant was changing into?"

"Yes, sir, I can. They were gray, the pajamas. Gray with black Darth Vader faces all over them."

"Did you say Darth Vader?"

"Yes, sir, I did."

"You mean the same Darth Vader that was on the defendant's sweatshirt when he took you into the back seat of his mother's car and suffocated you under his shirt?"

"Yup, that's the one, sir."

"Hmm." Scheck swiveled on his heel and looked right at me with one of those phony-suspicious kinds of looks.

He then turned back toward his witness.

"And what did the defendant do next?"

"Well, he kind of went in and out of the room a lot. Sounded a lot like sink and toilet sounds from what I could tell, so I think he was going back and forth from some sort of bathroom upstairs."

"Did the defendant brush his teeth that night, Mr. Banana?"

"Objection, Your Honor," said Bearbara.

"Overruled," said the plush owl.

Scheck repeated the question: "Did the defendant brush his teeth that night?"

"I'm not exactly sure, sir. I mean, I wasn't in the bathroom with him, but I do know that the sink went on and off quite a lot."

"Did the defendant tend to wash his hands a lot?"

"Objection," shouted Bearbara.

"Overruled," said the owl gruffly.

"I'm not really sure," said Bobby.

Scheck smirked at Bearbara and then turned back toward Bobby. "After the defendant finished his back-and-forth excursions to the bathroom, what happened then?"

"He turned the light back off in his bedroom."

"And then what happened?"

"He ran, and jumped onto the bed."

"Did he jump onto the *bed*, or did he jump onto one of the *plush animals* that was on the bed?"

"Well, since you put it that way, sir, I guess you could say he jumped onto Henry the Horse."

"Did you actually see him jump onto Henry the Horse?"

"I could sort of see it. It was pretty dark in the room other than the moonlight coming in through the window. But I could tell Henry the Horse was jumped on because he neighed really loud when it happened."

"Before we proceed any further, Mr. Banana, can you tell the jury who could hear these sounds that you or any of the other plush animals made at any time when you were occupying the defendant's bedroom?"

"Oh, that would be just the plush animals and the defendant, sir. No one else could have heard these sounds. Not even the defendant's mother or father, or sister even. The defendant was the only human being who could hear these sounds or words or sentences us plush animals living in his bedroom would make."

"And do you believe that this exception to the common laws of reality that the defendant had at his disposal as a child is still an exception in this courtroom today—that is, that the defendant is the only human being who could hear the sounds and words and sentences that you and your plush animal brethren have the capacity to make?"

"Yes, sir. I do."

"So despite this—I guess one could say—*privileged* gift that the defendant had, and continues to have, at his disposal, of being able to hear the pleas of mercy that you and the other plush animals made during those darkest hours in his bedroom—that still didn't stop him from what came next now, did it?"

"Objection, Your Honor!" Bearbara was so upset that he was frothing at the mouth.

Or maybe he was just hungry again for more plush honey.

"Sustained," said Judge Owl. "Mr. Scheck, I won't tell you again: you must restrain yourself from emotionally-charged and leading questions."

"Understood, Your Honor," said Scheck. "So, Mr. Banana—what happened after the defendant jumped onto Henry the Horse? Did the defendant apologize?"

"No, sir, he did not."

"Didn't even apologize." Scheck looked at me and shook his head. "So what did he do then?"

"He got into bed—under the covers, I mean."

"And then?"

"And then he—he—he put his hand under the covers."

"He put his hand under the covers?"

"Yes, sir."

"Which hand was it—was it his left hand or his right hand?"

"His left."

"And was the defendant on his back or on his stomach when he inserted his left hand under the covers?"

"On his back—or at least at first, I mean."

"At first?"

"Um, yeah. Hey, I'm sorry, but does anyone have a banana they can give me? I'm getting kind of hungry up here. Also, I tend to get pretty nervous when I have to speak in front of an audience, and when I get nervous, my mouth turns dry, and I begin to stutter."

"That's entirely understandable, Mr. Banana—especially given what you've had to experience and witness."

"Pardon me for asking the question, Mr. Banana," said Judge Owl, "but can you explain to the court how you expect to eat this banana if it were to be delivered to you, given that you have, in fact, no digestive tract in which to swallow and digest it?"

"Oh, I wouldn't actually eat the banana, Your Honor," said Bobby. "I would just put it in my mouth, gobble it into bits and pieces, and then let it all fall out of my mouth in order to create the illusion that I am eating a banana at a frenetic pace."

"You mean, sort of like Cookie Monster eating his cookies, right?"

"Um, I guess so. I never really thought of it that way. But, yeah."

"I see." The Wise Old Owl nodded his head at the clerk. The clerk was a jackass—a plush jackass, that is. The jackass placed a banana on the witness stand in front of Bobby, and Bobby grabbed it quickly and shoved it into his mouth. As he chomped on the banana, small chunks scattered just about everywhere but down his throat. When he finished his chomping, he scratched his armpit and let one go.

"Ready now, Mr. Banana?" said Scheck.

Bobby let one rip again, and then belched out another. "Ready, sir."

"So, what happened after the defendant put his left hand under the covers?"

"Well, it was then that we all started to bob up and down on the bed."

"When you say 'we,' do you mean you and the other plush animals on the defendant's bed?"

"That's correct."

"And what was causing this bobbing up and down?"

"His hand."

"The defendant's left hand?"

"Yes, sir."

"You mean the one that was under the covers?"

"Yes, sir."

"How long did this go on for, this bobbing up and down?"

"Probably like two minutes or so."

"Two minutes or so?"

"Yeah, two minutes—maybe three."

"And what happened after this bobbing up and down ended? Did the defendant fall asleep?"

"No, he did not, sir."

"What did the defendant do then instead?"

"He turned over on his belly."

"On his belly, you say?"

"Yes, sir."

"And then what happened?"

"He took his hand—I think it was his right hand—and snatched Mr. Shakesbear."

"When you say 'snatched' him, do you mean snatched him by the arm?"

"No, sir."

"By what then?"

"By the beret, sir."

"You mean the beret that you described as all but stripped from the sewn-in stitches on the top portion of his head?"

"Yes, sir. That's the one."

"And what did the defendant do after he snatched Mr. Shakesbear by the beret?"

"He brought him under the covers with him."

"And where exactly under the covers did the defendant place Mr. Shakesbear?"

"Under himself. Under near where his belly was."

"Under his belly?"

"Um, no—I mean, probably a little lower than his belly."

"You mean, like where his . . . *penis* would be?" Scheck did a little waltz halfway toward the jury box as if the very sound of the word *penis* made him dance.

"Objection," growled my grizzly attorney.

"Overruled," hooted the feathery judge.

"Mr. Banana," said Scheck. "Was it under his penis where the defendant placed Mr. Shakesbear?"

"Yes," said Bobby. "Around there, yes."

"So, the defendant's penis was on top of Mr. Shakesbear, with Mr. Shakesbear having to withstand the full suffocating and pulverizing weight of the defendant's pasty and bony body." Scheck turned to look at me with exaggerated revulsion, and then turned back to Bobby. "Did the defendant ever ask Mr. Shakesbear if he *wanted* to be placed under his penis?"

"No, he did not ask, sir."

"Would you say that this act committed by the defendant of placing Mr. Shakesbear under his penis—would you say it was a consensual act?"

"No, sir. I absolutely would not."

"Was the defendant naked while he had Mr. Shakesbear under his penis?"

"No, sir. He still had his pajamas on."

"You mean those Darth Vader pajamas, correct?"

"That is correct, sir."

"So then what happened?"

"Well, everything started to bob up and down on the bed again."

"You mean for you and the other plush animals on the defendant's bed?"

"Uh-huh. But this time, the bobbing up and down—well, it was a lot faster this time."

"And by 'a lot faster this time,' you mean a lot faster than when the defendant was on his back with only his left hand under the covers, correct?"

"Yes, sir. That's correct."

"Now, did the defendant say anything while he was bobbing up and down on Mr. Shakesbear with his penis?"

"Sir?"

"Did the defendant say anything—did he speak at all—while he had Mr. Shakesbear under his penis?"

"Well, yeah. He did. But I couldn't really make out much of what he was saying."

"Because?"

"Because half his face was in his pillow."

"Could you make out anything he said, anything at all?"

"Well, I sort of could. I know he said 'ginger' a lot."

"Ginger? As in the spice, ginger, or as in the female name, Ginger?"

"I'm not really sure, sir. I mean, I figured back then that he meant the spice, but hearing you now put it the other way, who knows?"

"Fair enough, Mr. Banana. Fair enough. So, this more frenetic bobbing up and down while Mr. Shakesbear was being held under the defendant's penis against his will—this nonconsensual act, as you pointed out—for how long did it go on?"

"For about three or four minutes, I would say."

"Three or four minutes. And during those three or four minutes, did Mr. Shakesbear ever say anything—anything at all—to the defendant or to anyone else while this was happening to him?"

"He did not, sir."

"Yet you say it was not consensual."

"That's right, sir."

"Then how come Mr. Shakesbear did not protest or defend himself against the defendant's actions?"

"It all happened so quickly, sir. I think it was because he was scared."

"Could it also be because he was being smothered by the force of the defendant's devastating weight and pelvic thrusts?"

"Yes. Probably that, too, sir."

"And so when those three or four minutes of bobbing up and down ended—"

"Well, it didn't really end there, sir."

"Come again?"

"The bobbing up and down—it didn't really end there. He just stopped for a bit."

"The defendant stopped for a bit, you say?"

"Yes, sir."

"You mean, he stopped for a bit because he was tired? Stopped for a bit because he was feeling remorseful? Stopped for a bit because he realized that what he was doing to Mr. Shakesbear was grossly wrong and morally reprehensible?"

"Well, um, no, sir."

"Then why did the defendant stop for a bit?"

"He stopped for a bit to pull back the covers from his body."

"So, the defendant pulled back the covers from his body."

"Yes, sir. He pulled back the covers and took each one of us plush animals, one by one, and stood each one of us up so that we could get a better view of what he was about to do."

"And what was the defendant about to do?"

"The same thing he was doing to Mr. Shakesbear before he pulled the covers off."

"You mean, that same thrusting of his penis into Mr. Shakesbear's body?"

"Yes, sir. That's correct."

"And how was Mr. Shakesbear positioned under the defendant's thrusting pelvic motions? In what position was Mr. Shakesbear's body placed?"

"He was placed on his back. It was kind of like his torso was getting pushed into over and over again. Not really sure why it was his torso. It was all very creepy."

"Very creepy, indeed." Scheck winked at one of the plush jurors. "And he forced all of you plush animals that were on his bed to watch this despicable act, yes?"

"Yes, sir."

"Did anyone tell him to stop?"

Bobby swallowed hard and his jaw began to tremble. "No. No, sir. None of us did. But only because we were all too scared. None of us wanted to be next."

"So, when the defendant was having forced sexual intercourse with Mr. Shakesbear, what was—"

"Objection, Your Honor!" blurted Bearbara. This time his belly hit the underside of the table, so he ended up remaining in his chair. "How could my client have 'forced sexual intercourse' with Mr. Shakesbear, as Mr. Scheck is asserting, when Mr. Shakesbear does not possess any sexual organ with which to even *have* sexual intercourse?"

Shakesbear glared at my attorney and sneered.

"Sustained," said Judge Owl.

"Very well then," said Scheck. "So, when the defendant was sexually assaulting Mr. Shakesbear, was he still wearing his pajamas?"

"Yes, sir," said Bobby.

"All the way up until sexual climax?"

"Yes, sir."

"Really?"

"Um, yeah. Yes, sir. He was. Really."

Scheck glanced over at me in genuinely disgusted disbelief, then turned uneasily back toward his witness.

I think this was new territory—even for Scheck.

"But these pajamas the defendant was wearing—were they not the Darth Vader pajamas you mentioned earlier?"

"Yes, sir. They were."

"And now they had become these very, very wet and very, very sticky Darth Vader pajamas, yes?"

Bobby stopped to think that over for a moment. "Um, yeah. I suppose so, sir."

"I appreciate your testimony, Mr. Banana. I could only imagine what you, Mr. Shakesbear, and your plush brethren had to endure in that dark, dark bedroom. You were very brave to share your experience with us here today. Thank you. I have no further questions, Your Honor."

The Wise Old Owl looked at my attorney. "Your witness, Counsel."

Bearbara managed to fully stand up this time before lumbering his way over to the front of the witness stand.

"Good morning, Mr. Banana."

"Good morning, sir."

"Going back to that first day—and by the way, I, too, appreciate your testimony here today—but going back to that first day, that day you were purchased and first taken to my client's childhood home in his mother's car, did you say that you had trouble breathing under my client's sweatshirt in the back seat?"

"Yes, I did say that."

"And how is that?"

"How is what, sir?"

"I mean, how is it that you, a plush animal with no real respiratory organs to speak of—how would you ever have any trouble breathing when the act of breathing is not even a viable option for an individual with your physical properties?"

Bobby jumped out of his seat. "Hey, man, I can breathe, okay?"

"Can you?" Bearbara took out a small pocket mirror from the inside of his extra-extra-extra-large pinstriped suit jacket and put it in front of Bobby's face. "Mr. Banana, if you would be so kind, could you please exhale into this mirror?"

"Sir?"

"Mr. Banana, if you really can breathe as you say you can, this mirror in front of you will fog up when you breathe out, correct?"

"This is absurd!"

"Perhaps it is absurd, Mr. Banana. But you must breathe out regardless."

Bobby looked glumly at the judge, but the Wise Old Owl nodded sternly at him to oblige my attorney's instruction. Bobby then took what appeared to be a deep breath and blew out as hard as he could at the mirror.

Nothing appeared on the glass—or so it seemed.

The spectators gasped in unison.

Bobby hung his head. I actually felt a little bad for him.

Bearbara did his own little fat-bear kind of waltz to the jury box. "Let the record show that Mr. Banana has exhibited no evidence of respiration and is therefore incapable of breathing, and insomuch that he is incapable of breathing, he is incapable of suffering under my client's sweatshirt, or under anyone's sweatshirt for that matter, and therefore has perjured himself!"

"Objection, Your Honor!" roared Scheck.

"Overruled!" screeched Judge Owl, banging his gavel down.

"Your Honor," said Bearbara. "Since Mr. Banana has obviously discredited himself, the defense wishes to have all testimony of his removed from evidence and— "

"But I can breathe!" cried Bobby. "I really can! Now, maybe you can't see it. Maybe the jury can't see it. And maybe even Judge Owl can't see it either. But *he* can!" He pointed his finger right at me. "That no-good bastard sure can! He can hear and see everything that we plush animals say and do! And that's what's relevant here."

Judge Owl banged his gavel down again. "*I* will decide what is relevant and not relevant in this courtroom, Mr. Banana. Not you!"

"Your Honor," said Scheck. He was smirking again, for he had yet another trick up his sleeve. "Your Honor, I think we should hear the witness out on his claim. If his contention is true, then the defendant should see evidence of respiration on the pocket mirror his attorney has presented. If not, well, then I guess the witness's testimony should be dismissed after all."

The Wise Old Owl paused for a moment or two to consider Scheck's suggestion, and then cleared his throat. "Well, given that what is relevant here is what the witness perceived and what the defendant perceived and not what a third party would have perceived, I am going to instruct that the defendant take a look at his attorney's pocket mirror and report if he sees any evidence of respiration. I would remind the defendant that he is under oath."

My attorney shook his head and muttered under his breath, and then reluctantly allowed me a look at his pocket mirror.

It looked all fogged up to me. I nodded my head meekly.

Judge Owl looked at me with surprise. "Well then! I guess I owe Mr. Banana an apology. Plush members of the jury, let the record show that the defendant has identified evidence of respiration on the pocket mirror from the witness. I will therefore instruct the defendant's attorney to proceed in his cross-examination."

Bearbara glared at Scheck and then cleared his throat. "Thank you, Your Honor. Mr. Banana, when you arrived at my client's childhood home so many years ago, you said that he carried you up the stairs to his bedroom and then left you in the dark with the other plush animals—is that correct?"

"That's correct, sir. Yes."

"And then you said that the beret that had been sewn onto the head of Mr. Shakesbear was hanging by a single stitch, and that Mr. Shakesbear looked tired and quite sad—'depressed' is what I think you said."

"Yes, sir. That's what I said. Depressed. Very depressed."

"But you also said it was dark inside the bedroom. Very dark."

"Yes, I did say that, too, sir. It *was* dark. *Very* dark."

"But how could you assess or even see Mr. Shakesbear's condition if it was so dark?"

"Well, I couldn't see one-hundred-percent clear, but—"

"Say that again."

"I said, I couldn't see one-hundred-percent clear, but—"

"You couldn't see one-hundred-percent clear." Bearbara turned to face the jury. "You couldn't see one-hundred-percent clear." He turned back toward Bobby. "Mr. Banana, would it not be fair to say then that based on your claim—a claim that you have made under oath in this courtroom today—that you could not see one-hundred-percent clear in the extreme dark of my client's childhood bedroom, that there is absolutely no way you can be one-hundred-percent certain that Mr. Shakesbear was in the emotional and physical condition you claimed he was in?"

"Well, I guess—"

"Objection, Your Honor!" shouted Scheck.

"Overruled," said the plush owl. "The witness will answer the question."

Bobby started to scratch his hairy armpits and torso again. "Well, I guess all I was saying was—"

"Mr. Banana." My attorney leaned a paw on the witness stand, making it creak. His enormous size obstructed just about everyone's view of the witness. "Can you claim, under oath, with one-hundred-percent certainty, the true state of Mr. Shakesbear's emotional and physical condition in that dark, dark bedroom way back in 1982?"

Bobby let out a deep sigh into the witness microphone. "One-hundred-percent? No, sir, I can't make that claim."

"And can you therefore claim, under oath, with one-hundred-percent certainty, that my client sexually assaulted Mr. Shakesbear under the covers, when, not only was your sight impeded by the dark, but also by two layers of bedclothes?"

Bobby looked at Scheck, and Scheck responded with a reluctant nod of his head.

"No, sir," said Bobby. "Not one-hundred-percent."

"Thank you, Mr. Banana. I appreciate your honesty. I have no further questions, Your Honor."

"Thank you, Mr. Banana," said the Wise Old Owl. "You may step down from the witness stand. The prosecution may call its next witness."

Scheck stood up. "The prosecution calls Mr. William Shakesbear to the stand."

The courtroom oohed and aahed. Shakesbear bowed to the spectators sitting behind him and pranced his way over to the witness stand.

"State your name," said the jackass clerk.

"William Shakesbear."

"Mr. Shakesbear," said the jackass, "do you swear to tell the truth, the whole truth and nothing but the truth, so help you God?"

"Aye, good sir."

Judge Owl leaned toward Shakesbear. "What was that you said, Mr. Shakesbear?"

"I said, 'Aye, good sir.' "

"Mr. Shakesbear, please answer with a 'yes' or a 'no.' "

"Very well, my Lord. Yes, I say."

"And please address me as 'Your Honor' or 'Judge Owl.' "

"Aye, Your Honor. Um, I mean, er, yes."

"Mr. Shakesbear, thank you for your willingness to take the stand here today," said Scheck. "I'm sure, as you've been sitting here in this courtroom, listening to the various testimonies of this case, that you have been champing at the bit to offer your own true account. Of course, you, as much as anyone sitting in this courtroom today, have been a target of the defendant's violent sexual aggression. We are glad you are here today to share with us some of the facts about what transpired."

" 'Tis a pleasure and a noble honor, sir."

"So, when and how did you meet the defendant?"

"Our stars first crossed about two scores ago. His mother set forth our introduction."

"And how did the defendant's mother know you?"

"My lady was my first keeper, sir."

"You mean his mother was your guardian, correct?"

"Aye. Yes. Precisely, sir."

"And at some point, that guardianship was transferred over to the defendant—is that correct?"

"It is."

"Did the defendant's mother ever say *why* that guardianship was transferred?"

"Nay, sir. Nought a reason was uttered, though I imagine it had much to do with her excessive collection of V.I.B.s."

"V.I.B.s?"

"Very Important Bears. It was a series of plush bears manufactured by the North American Bear Company during the 1980s and '90s based on human beings who had attained a certain level of fame." He looked over at my attorney. "Or notoriety, I suppose."

"Who were some of these other Very Important Bears, or V.I.B.s, under the defendant's mother's guardianship?"

"Hmm, let me recall ... There was Scarlett O'Beara, Carmen Bearanda, Kareem Abdul-Jabbear, Bearilyn Monroe, Marlon Bearando, Libearace, Beary Manilow, Blackbear'd, The Statue of Libearty, Abearham Lincoln, Ludwig Von Bearthoveen, Beartolt Brecht—oh, and Bearistotle, of course. Several others, too, if my memory serves me well."

"That's a lot of Very Important Bears for one household."

" 'Tis, indeed."

"Yet none of those other Very Important Bears were later placed under the guardianship of the defendant—is that correct?"

"Well, nary a bear except one. It is my understanding that before either the defendant's mother or the defendant claimed guardianship of me that Amelia Bearhart had been passed on to the defendant by his mother just before an extended excursion to the village where his grandparents resided, down near the southern beaches of Florida. From what I hear from others is that Lady Bearhart went inexplicably missing when the defendant's belongings were retrieved at baggage claim at Palm Beach International. She was never found."

"Did the defendant ever try to find his missing Amelia Bearhart?"

"No, sir. He did not."

The courtroom let out another collective gasp. Turning in my chair, I could see Bucky the One-Eyed Bunny in the audience, shaking his head. Looking at him, I could still remember when he had two eyes, back before I had accidentally gouged one of them out with the spasmodic thrusts of my—

The Wise Old Owl banged his gavel down. "Order. Order in the court. Alright then, please proceed, Mr. Scheck."

"Mr. Shakesbear," said Scheck, "if the defendant was so irresponsible and negligent and who-knows-what-else toward Ms. Bearhart, why would the defendant's mother have ever transferred her guardianship of you over to the defendant?"

"Oh, you see, sir, I was never really 'transferred,' as you say, over to the defendant."

"You were never transferred over to him?"

"Nay, sir. I was kidnapped by him."

"Kidnapped?"

"Aye, kidnapped. And with the plethora of V.I.B.s under her guardianship, methinks the defendant's mother was never even aware of my disappearance from her shelf. It makes my heart heavy, even after all these years, that I had never left the impression on his mother that I thought I had made. Oh, woe is me!"

"Now, now, Mr. Shakesbear. I'm sure you made some sort of impression. After all, you are the legendary William Shakesbear, the North American Bear Company version of the greatest playwright and most influential literary figure who ever lived."

"Why, thank you, sir. Thy kind words are taken with utmost solace and gratitude."

"In fact, if you can sign my copy of King Bear—"

Bearbara shot up from his chair, knocking the counsel table over with his oversized gut. "Objection, Your Honor!"

"Sustained," said Judge Owl. "Mr. Scheck, will you please stay focused on the proceedings of this case?"

"Apologies, Your Honor," said Scheck. "Now, Mr. Shakesbear, can you please describe for us how you were treated by the defendant during your earliest encounters with him?"

"Aye, sir. He was mostly kind, I suppose." Shakesbear thought for a moment.

"Mr. Shakesbear? Is something wrong?"

"Well, come to think of it, he did have a strange way of touching me, even during those earliest of days."

"How did he touch you?"

"Well, he never really touched *me* too much, one could say, but rather my blouse."

"Your blouse?"

"Yes, he seemed to be taken with its texture."

"And what sort of texture was that?"

"That of satin."

"That of Satan?"

"Nay, sir. Satin—that of satin, is what I said."

"So, the defendant had perhaps some sort of fetish for Satan—I mean satin, yes?

"If not satin in general, then at least my satin blouse in particular, aye."

"This satin blouse you speak of—is this the same satin blouse you are wearing today in this court-room?"

"Aye, sir."

"Now, Mr. Shakesbear, we will definitely get back to your satin blouse in just a moment, but for now, can you tell us if you can recall the first night the defendant took you into his childhood bedroom?"

"Aye, sir. I can recall it."

"Can you describe the defendant's bedroom, how it was that first night?"

"Aye, sir. 'Twas dark. 'Twas very dark and very humid. The air conditioning unit, I fear, did not perform the way it was intended to perform."

"But you still could see the defendant in this very dark room, yes?"

"Aye, sir. The moonlight through the bedroom window made it so."

"What was the defendant wearing that night?"

"A Darth Vader pajama top and a pair of Darth Vader underoos, sir."

"Darth Vader underoos?"

"Aye, sir. Or at least that is what I deduced from the black and gray colors of his underoos, which bore a likeness to the colors of his Darth Vader pajama top."

"And this first night he brought you into his bedroom—did he also bring you over to his bed?"

"Aye, sir."

"Can you describe the bed?"

"Aye, sir. It was a twin bed with 'Empire Strikes Back' bedsheets and a navy-blue comforter."

"And during that first night in his bedroom, did the defendant ever take you under the covers with him?"

"Aye, sir. He did."

"And did the defendant ever touch you when you were under the covers with him?"

"Aye, sir. He did."

"How did the defendant touch you?"

"He rubbed me back and forth over his loins."

"And when he rubbed you back and forth over his loins, did you ever tell him to stop?"

"Nay, sir. I could not."

"You could not tell him to stop? Why was that?"

"Well, I had trouble breathing underneath the covers, of course—let alone my capacity for utterance under the circumstances."

"What part of your body was he rubbing against when he rubbed you back and forth over his loins?"

"My torso, if only my torso was not covered by my blouse."

"You mean your *satin* blouse, correct?"

"Aye, sir."

"The one you are wearing here today in this courtroom, yes?"

" 'Tis the one."

"Now, Mr. Shakesbear, did the defendant ever make an attempt to remove your satin blouse that night?"

"Nay, sir."

"Did he ever make an attempt to remove your satin blouse on any night or on any occasion at all?"

"Nay, sir."

"So, after the defendant rubbed you back and forth over his loins during that first night in his bedroom, what did he do then?"

"He turned over on his belly, and then shoved me *under* his loins."

"So now you've gone from being over his loins to under his loins, correct?"

"Aye, sir."

"And when the defendant had you under his loins, was he still wearing his Darth Vader underoos?"

"Aye, sir."

"And when he had you under his loins with his Darth Vader underoos still on, what did he do then?"

"He started mounting me, to and fro."

"To and fro?"

"Aye, sir. To and fro, and hither and thither."

"Hither and thither?"

"Hither and thither."

"How long did this to-and-fro and hither-and-thither situation go on for?"

"For a few minutes or so. Until he finished the final act."

"Until he finished the final act? When you say 'finished the final act,' do you mean 'act' as in Act Three, like in one of your plays?"

"Not an act of that sort, nay. By 'finished the final act,' I mean until he reached his own, er—how shall I say it?—romantic climax."

"And by 'romantic climax,' you mean the moment of ejaculation, yes?"

"Ejaculation sounds too merry a word for what was done upon me, but aye—ejaculation it was."

"And did the defendant ejaculate on you through his Darth Vader underoos, Mr. Shakesbear?"

"If you count my satin blouse as part of who I am, then aye."

"And how many times, would you say, did the defendant ejaculate on you in such a manner over the years?"

"Once every night for the first fortnight, and then about twice every day hence till he turned eleven years."

"Twice a day?"

"Aye. Sometimes even thrice."

"*Thrice?*"

Scheck shook his head at me, then turned back toward Shakesbear.

"Mr. Shakesbear, I am so sorry that you had to undergo such pain and suffering for so long. Unfortunately, there are so many other plush animals who have shared a similar fate at the hands, and other anatomical parts, of the defendant, many of whom are in this very courtroom at this very moment. On behalf of all those victims and sufferers, I say thank you for sharing your testimony with us today. Your Honor, I have no further questions."

"Your witness, Mr. Bearbara," said the Wise Old Owl.

"Mr. Shakesbear," said Bearbara, breathing heavily. He didn't even bother trying to get up from his chair this time, he was so winded. "I'd like to resume where Mr. Scheck left off. Now, you told the courtroom that my client ejaculated on your satin blouse multiple times a day for several years, yes?"

"Aye, sir."

"Well, if my client ejaculated on your satin blouse multiple times a day for several years, and you are now wearing that very same satin blouse that was ejaculated on, how come there is not a single stain from ejaculation present on that blouse today in this courtroom?"

Shakesbear slumped down in his chair and began to squirm.

Bearbara went in for the kill. "Mr. Shakesbear, can you point out to the jury any and all stains from ejaculation that are present on the blouse you are wearing today in this courtroom?"

Shakesbear's head sunk down into his paws and offered no reply.

"Well, Mr. Shakesbear?" said Bearbara. "We're waiting."

Shakesbear's mouth was trembling, unable to speak. I prayed for it not to be able to speak ever again.

"Your Honor," said Bearbara, "I have no further questions. The defense rests." He pinched the lapels of his suit jacket with satisfaction and winked at me with assurance. This case was in the bag, said his wink.

"Your Honor," said Scheck, "I wish for a redirect."

"Granted," said the plush owl.

"Thank you, Your Honor. Mr. Shakesbear? Mr. Shakesbear. Would you care to explain to the jury why there is no evidence of ejaculation—why there are no 'stains from ejaculation,' as Mr. Bearbara just phrased it—on your satin blouse today? Please, Mr. Shakesbear. The jury, this courtroom—we all know this must be hard for you, but we all also want to hear your side of the story. You owe it to justice. You owe it to all the victims. You owe it to yourself."

Shakesbear lifted his head and looked at Scheck. His mouth was still trembling, but his eyes were focused and determined.

"Aye, sir. I do care to explain. The reason wherefore the stains you speak of are not present on my satin blouse is rooted in yet another trauma that the defendant inflicted upon me."

"And what trauma is that, Mr. Shakesbear?"

"Well, it happened about a week or so ago—shortly after the defendant's mother passed away."

Bearbara looked at me with panicked bewilderment. He had no clue what was coming, but I sure did.

"Go on, Mr. Shakesbear," said Scheck. "Continue."

"Well, as perhaps you are aware," said Shakesbear, "the defendant—and by 'the defendant,' I of course mean Mr. Kornreich—paid a visit to the residence of his youth right after his mother's funeral. I believe it was on the occasion of family, friends and other mourners of the deceased sitting shiva on the ground floor of the house."

Bearbara turned to me with his jaw dropped. "How come you didn't tell me about this?" he whispered.

I shrugged my shoulders sheepishly and hung my head. I had been too ashamed to let him know.

"I suspect he took it upon himself to empty out his mother's storage closet," continued Shakesbear. "An inebriated wreck, he was, the poor soul. I am sure he missed his mother dearly." He looked directly at me, with utmost tenderness. "I am sure he still misses her now."

And there he was: Shakesbear, the legendary-plush-playwright-turned-master-plush-thespian. Probably his best performance yet.

"So what happened, Mr. Shakesbear?" said Scheck. "What happened when the defendant went upstairs to empty out his mother's storage closet?"

Shakesbear looked back at Scheck. "He spied me in the back corner of the closet. I had been sitting atop a stack of his mother's old Cat Stevens records for years, abandoned and neglected. It had seemed like eons since I had witnessed any inkling of daylight. I was thick with dust. It all felt like a dream when he opened that closet door." Shakesbear's gaze went over the heads of all the spectators in the courtroom. "In fact, it still does feel like a dream. A horrific dream, no doubt."

Shakesbear's voice had become a whisper.

So became Scheck's as well. "Go on, Mr. Shakes-bear. Please. Go on."

Shakesbear gulped and then continued: "He saw me sitting in that dark corner of the storage closet, and that is when the heaviness in his eyes, in the shortest of blinks, gave way to a lucid twinkle. It was as if we both had a mutual understanding of the moment. It was as if finding each other again, in this serendipitous way, after so many years, lib-erated us both, that whatever happened between us so long ago had become water under the bridge, as they say."

"What happened then, Mr. Shakesbear?" whis-pered Scheck, as he licked his lips. "What happened then?"

Shakesbear glared at me with his beady black eyes. "Well, I suppose the understanding was only mine, for he grabbed me by the beret and flung me onto his mother's bed."

The courtroom groaned in horror.

Shakesbear continued, looking squarely at the jury now. "He began to undress. He was like a mad-man! He tried removing his necktie, but it was too difficult for him to finesse, so instead he took off his shoes and kicked them aside. Then he unbuck-led his belt buckle, pushed down his pants, and tossed those aside as well. Then he—he—he—"

"What happened, Mr. Shakesbear? What did the defendant do next?"

Shakesbear snapped his head back and shut his eyes. "He *ravished* me! That satin-worshipping devil of a man! He ravished me!"

"With his underpants still on?"

"Aye!" Shakesbear opened his eyes with a sinister grin and gazed in my direction. "Aye, they were still on, indeed!"

Bearbara covered his eyes with his paws. *Mayday. Mayday.* Our ship was sinking, and Scheck was withholding all the life jackets, waving them in front of our noses.

"For how long did the defendant ravish you?"

"About thirty seconds. Forty perhaps. A quickie by any standard. But it seemed like thirty or forty days and nights to me!" Shakesbear rubbed his eyes and sobbed. "Oh, the wounds! The wounds this bear-heart bears!"

"Did the defendant say anything during this savage sexual assault? Did he say why he was doing this to you?"

"Nay. He never said why. All he kept saying was 'Yes, God, oh! Yes, God, oh!' and 'Juliet! Juliet! Juliet!' Mocking me with one of my very own fictional characters, he was!"

"That's a lie!" I shouted.

"Mr. Kornreich!" The Wise Old Owl slammed his gavel down. "I will not allow you to speak out of turn in my courtroom. Consider yourself warned. Proceed, Counsel."

Scheck continued: "So, the defendant said the Lord's name in vain while he assaulted you?"

"Aye, sir. He most certainly did, indeed!"

"And at the end of this horrific and blasphemous assault, did he ejaculate on your satin blouse?"

"Oh, yes—just like old times!" Shakesbear dropped his face into his paws again and resumed his sobbing.

"And with his underpants still on, correct?"

"Aye-aye." Shakesbear took out a handkerchief from the pocket of his trousers to wipe away his tears—that is, if there really *were* any real tears to wipe.

"Mr. Shakesbear," said Scheck, "I am so sorry that you had to withstand yet even more punishing trauma from this—this—" Scheck jabbed his pointed finger in my direction. "—this lowlife of a defendant." He turned his attention back toward Shakesbear. "But as traumatic as that experience must have been for you, that still does not explain why there's no evidence of ejaculation present on the satin blouse that you are wearing today in this courtroom. Can you please explain to the jury why that is so?"

"Aye, sir. I can explain. I can, and I shall."

Shakesbear paused and watched me squirm in my chair. He knew he had me set up for the knockout—I could see it in the glint of his black marble eyes. All he had to do was deliver the final blow.

And deliver he did.

Shakesbear paused for a moment more, opened his mouth, then spoke: "He drowned me." His words echoed over the courtroom as if they had been delivered from somewhere up above.

The jury was aghast. So, too, was the Honorable Judge Owl. They couldn't believe their furry and feathery ears.

"Excuse me, Mr. Shakesbear," said Scheck. "Did you just say the defendant drowned you?"

"Aye," said Shakesbear. "After he had unloaded himself upon my satin blouse, he inserted me in his mother's laundry machine, and drowned me in the most frigid of wash modes, in the dankest of laundry rooms, in the mustiest of basements, and after a good thirty minutes, retrieved my drenched body, before burning me to a crisp in his mother's dryer."

"Dear God," whispered one of the plush jurors.

"For how long were you being burned alive in his mother's dryer, Mr. Shakesbear?" said Scheck.

"Forty-five minutes, most likely. But I cannot say with any precise degree of certainty, for I had already passed out about ten minutes in."

"Why didn't the defendant just take your blouse off, and then wash it and dry it that way?"

"Perhaps he would have." Shakesbear glanced at me. "If he had any decency, that is." He turned back toward Scheck. "But the choice was not his to make. Nay, that choice had already been made by the North American Bear Company when they designed me in their studio: like many of my bearish brethren, my blouse was sewn onto my velvet skin. I guess my creator never foresaw such depravity from a fellow human."

"So, Mr. Shakesbear, when you awoke from your trauma-induced state of unconsciousness, where were you? Was the defendant still in the basement with you?"

"Well, I was, in fact, still semi-unconscious at the time his mother's housekeeper found me inside the dryer. I am not exactly certain why she was present in the residence that afternoon. Perhaps to put away all the leftovers from the shiva call? Or perhaps to tidy up the house before the defendant put it on the market? I cannot definitively say. But when I regained full consciousness and peered into her gentle brown eyes, I could see that she was both confused and quite frightened by having found me in the dryer of her deceased employer. Nevertheless, she carried me up two flights of stairs in order to put me back into that storage closet—back into that dark corner atop that same stack of old Cat Stevens records."

Scheck nodded. "And you're still sitting in that dark corner of the storage closet right now, at this very moment, on top of that same stack of old Cat Stevens records, yes?"

"Aye, sir. I sit atop that same stack of old Cat Stevens records at this very moment just as I sit in the very same instant in this very courtroom that occupies Mr. Kornreich's malicious and loathsome imagination. I sit both hither and thither at once, and bask in the glow of his guilty conscience."

Scheck let it all sink in for the jury for a moment or two, and then he put on the finishing touches. "Mr. Shakesbear, again, thank you so very much for sharing your testimony with us today. I think everyone in this courtroom—except perhaps the defendant and his counsel—would agree that this sort of deviant behavior that human beings inflict upon their plush animals—this nonconsensual plush bestiality, if you will—should no longer be tolerated. If anyone has ever wondered about how our nation's college campuses have devolved into a culture of rape and degradation, how our society has become a circus overrun by violent and sadistic fetishes, look no further than the human-made home, for inside every one of those homes there is a bedroom in which the rapists and predators of the future are being incubated, lurking in the shadows, ravishing, objectifying, and defiling our soft and inanimate bodies without any thought of our consent. They're using us as sexual target practice is what they're doing—sexual target practice for their cruel and repugnant impulses—*childish* impulses that they never seem to fully outgrow." Scheck turned back toward Shakesbear. "Mr. Shakesbear, thank you so much for your time. I hope that your testimony, and the testimony of the other witnesses, will send a clear message and be a first step in moving our nation, and perhaps humankind, toward a higher moral standard. Your Honor, I have no further questions. The prosecution rests."

Shakesbear stood up in the witness box. Before exiting the box stage right, he bowed first to the jury, and then to the rest of the courtroom, his beret flopping up and down on the soft velvet skin of his cherry-red scalp by a single stitch. As he made his usual dramatic gestures, both the jury and the spectators delivered a standing ovation.

Judge Owl had to bang his gavel down several times before order was restored.

I looked at the empty chair next to me. My attorney was no longer in the courtroom.

"As there is no further witness testimony from either side, we can now begin with the closing arguments. Mr. Kornreich, what say you?"

With my lawyer having bailed on me, I was too scared and too ashamed to speak on my own behalf. I just looked at the judge and shook my head.

"Mr. Kornreich, are you sure you have nothing to say for yourself? This is the last opportunity to counter the accusations made against you."

I looked over at the jury.

I looked over at the empty chair that had been occupied by my attorney.

I looked over at Shakesbear, who was now lending me his fluffy red ears I had once cherished so much.

I felt so betrayed.

Looking back at the jury, I rose from my chair. It was hard for me to think at that moment, let alone speak, so I said the first thought that came to my head: "The first thing I'd like to say is this: Let's kill all the lawyers."

The courtroom gasped, and then hissed in disgust.

Shakesbear shook his head. "How low of you to pilfer from my theatrical repertoire and sully my very own words in such despicable fashion!"

"*Your* theatrical repertoire? *Your* very own words?" I sneered at him. "They're not *your* words. They're probably not even the *real* Shakespeare's words, for that matter, you pathetic excuse for a knock-off! So, why don't you just go fuck yourself—that is, if you actually have the anatomical properties to even *go* fuck yourself, of course!"

Judge Owl banged his gavel down so hard that the head of it came flying off the handle. "How dare you speak that way in my courtroom, Mr. Kornreich! I could hold you in contempt, but instead I'm just going to rescind the rest of your allotted time to defend yourself."

Brimming with confidence, Scheck delivered his closing argument. The jury seemed to nod their heads at everything he said.

Judge Owl gave the jury its instructions for deliberation, and after about the same time it took for me to make my cum disappear from Shakesbear's satin blouse, the jury returned with a verdict.

Guilty. Of all charges. Guilty of everything to the first degree.

The courtroom erupted with cheers and applause. Shakesbear hopped onto the counsel table and bowed again and again, beckoning for further and further exaltation.

The Honorable Judge Owl, without a working gavel at his disposal, banged himself dizzy with his beak until order was restored once again. Declaring that he would be flying south for the winter the next day, he decided to sentence me right then and there: death by beheading.

An owl flying south for the winter?

Death by beheading?

My heart rolled down to my toes.

My mother rolled over in her grave.

* * *

ON THE DAY of my public execution, they chained my hands and feet in cuffs made of that same plastic material that they use for wiffle ball bats. A young plush bear named Bear Mitzvah sang the Kaddish over and over in my prison cell, and as I was led to the chopping block, I couldn't help but notice that his tallis was made of satin.

I won't deny it: I wanted to fuck Bear Mitzvah's brains out right then and there. As I trudged on toward my demise, I wondered if anyone noticed the modest protuberance that had taken shape inside my orange death row jumpsuit.

With my head on the chopping block, I gazed out at the throng of onlookers. I could have sworn I spotted Amelia Bearhart standing in the middle of the crowd, chatting it up with Charles Lindbeargh while nodding in my direction. Guess someone had finally found her.

Some plush bigfoot from the execution squad covered my head with a hood. Even with my face and ears covered though, I could still hear someone out in the crowd shouting, "Off with his head! Off with his head!" I think it was Richard the Rhino, but I guess I'll never know for sure.

As Bear Mitzvah prayed for what he prayed, I prayed for a quick death but got something better: the axe that the masked executioner used to chop my head off was made out of nerf, courtesy of Fisher-Price. Though the executioner proceeded with pounding away at the back of my neck regardless, and continues to do so as I type these words out onto the page, his efforts haven't hurt me none, and after a few good whacks, the hood that had covered my head has slipped off, and I am now able to see the world more clearly for what it is. Sort of reminds me of that old saying Shakesbear used to always whisper in the dark in that brief moment between my nightly climax and my nocturnal unconsciousness: *All's well that ends well.*

'Tis true, my fair Shakesbear. 'Tis true, indeed.

Acknowledgments

A THUNDEROUS OVATION of thanks is owed to Jacob Smullyan and his Sagging Meniscus Press for allowing this fiction a fair hearing and then some. Also, bear-hugs and bear-kisses to my wife, Jennifer, and our two darling cubs, Zachary and Samuel, for reconnecting me to the old wonders of bed-time, and for introducing me to some newer ones as well.

JOSHUA KORNREICH is the author of *The Boy Who Killed Caterpillars* (Marick, 2007; Dzanc, 2013); *Knotty, Knotty, Knotty* (Black Mountain, 2014); *Horsebuggy* (Sagging Meniscus, 2019); *Cavanaugh* (Sagging Meniscus, 2021); and *Shakes Bear in the Dark* (Sagging Meniscus, 2022). He lives in New York City with his wife and two sons.

BLANK PAGE BOOKS

are dedicated to the memory of Royce M. Becker,
who designed Sagging Meniscus books from 2015–2020.

They are:

IVÁN ARGÜELLES
THE BLANK PAGE

JESI BENDER
KINDERKRANKENHAUS

MARVIN COHEN
BOOBOO ROI
THE HARD LIFE OF A STONE, AND OTHER THOUGHTS

GRAHAM GUEST
HENRY'S CHAPEL

JOSHUA KORNREICH
CAVANAUGH
SHAKES BEAR IN THE DARK

STEPHEN MOLES
YOUR DARK MEANING, MOUSE

M.J. NICHOLLS
CONDEMNED TO CYMRU

PAOLO PERGOLA
RESET

BARDSLEY ROSENBRIDGE
SORRY, I BROKE YOUR PROMISE

CHRISTOPHER CARTER SANDERSON
THE SUPPORT VERSES